The Trek
and
other stories

The Trek
and
other stories

Lawrence Hoba

WEAVER

PRESS

Published by
Weaver Press, Box A1922, Avondale, Harare. 2009

'The First Trek – the Pioneers' and 'The Second Trek – Going Home'
was first published as 'The Trek' in *Writing Now*, Weaver Press, 2005
'Specialisation' was first published in *Laughing Now*, Weaver Press,
2007

Typeset by Weaver Press
Cover Photograph: Wide Angle
Cover Design: Danes Design
Printed by Sable Press, Harare

The publishers would like to express their gratitude to HIVOS
for the support they have given to
Weaver Press in the development of their
fiction programme.

ISBN: 978 1 77922 100 1

Lawrence Hoba was born in 1983 in Masvingo. He studied Tourism and Hospitality Management at the University of Zimbabwe. He represents a new generation of young writers working hard to have their voices heard but recognises that writing is more art than impulse. Hoba's short stories and poetry have appeared in the *Mirror*, a magazine published by the Budding Writers of Zimbabwe, and various blogsites including <www.zimbablog.com>.

Contents

The First Trek – the Pioneers

THE OLD SCOTCH CART MAKES ITS WAY SLOWLY along the old beaten down track. 'J J Magudu, Zimuto' lies scribbled on both sides in black paint against the dark rotting wood. The inscription must be as old as the wood on which it lies. I do not know who wrote it. Even *baba* does not know because one day I asked him and he said that only his father, who is dead, knew about it. The axle is almost broken and the old metal wheels, brown with rust, make a squealing sound.

Baba sits on the edge of the cart, brandishing a long leather whip he occasionally cracks to urge the cattle pulling the cart on. Sometimes, when we are at home he uses it on *mhama*. It is the cow that is the problem. It stops frequently to feed her calf that is walking beside it. The ox, black with a white patch on his head, walks energetically; it has no suckling worries. It stares straight ahead, wearing the same expression as *baba* – tired and bored.

Sweat trickles down *baba's* face. Perched on his head is a broad-brimmed straw hat. *Mhama* wears one too and so do I. Only baby Chido doesn't. I know *mhama* will weave her one when she is old enough to wear a hat. *Baba* has a pair of *manyatera* and yellow overalls written 'NRZ' at the back. He never worked with the railways, he just brought the overalls home one evening. Mother never asked how he got them. Once she asked where he found the old pair of trousers he's wearing right now, and the answer she got was a swollen eye.

Mhama sits with her back to *baba*, staring at the road behind, her face expressionless. She does not even smile at baby Chido playing gleefully on her lap. She just holds her, to keep her from slipping. *Mhama* always goes to church on Sundays.

The church is an old building with a thatched roof that leaks when it rains. The roof should have been repaired long back, but there are not enough men to do the job. The preacher is an old fellow with broad square-rimmed spectacles and a beard that makes him look like a he-goat. I do not know why women cry when he preaches.

The sun is hot, Chido wails, *mhama* plants one big breast into her mouth, and she sucks happily. I am also hungry. *Mhama* gives me a gourd of sour milk to drink. Some pots and pans lie clattering in a corner. I hate the noise. A sack of maize meal, almost empty, sits next to the pots, in an old 20-litre tin. *Mhama* uses the tin to fetch water from the well every day, for washing Chido's old nappies, for cooking sadza and *muriwo*, and for father's bath. I always go down to the river to bath. A stool and some straw and hide mats sit in another corner. Father says women and children should not sit on stools. Sometimes when he's not at home, I sit on the stool. It shakes and squeaks. He must be afraid we will break it.

An old mattress lies rolled up with some blankets inside, tied with *gudza* rope, next to the mats. There is no bed base. Father erects one with sticks dug into the ground. My own bed, which we left behind, had a mattress made from sacks filled with soft straw. *Mhama* must have emptied the sacks and put them somewhere because I cannot see them from where I sit next to her.

Some old sacks lie next to the rolled mattress, they contain all our clothing. A few old nappies for Chido, *mhama*'s dresses, *baba*'s trousers and shirts, and my torn shorts and T-shirts. There is also *baba*'s old suit that he wears on special occasions.

A plough sits at the far end of the scotch cart, still looking new. *Mhama* bought it last year with money from her groundnuts. Though *mhama* always works hard, I prefer to play with Chido and *baba* favours the calabash. Two hoes lie next to the plough, *mhama*'s hoe is worn from use, *baba*'s is still new and clean. The inscription 'Master Farmer' is still visible. The only use his hoe is put to is rubbing against the shoulders when he goes to the fields to inspect the work that has been done.

A metal board leans against the plough, 'Mr B. J. Magudu, Black Commercial Farmer, Farm 24' is crudely scribbled in white paint. I had never known *baba* wanted to be a commercial farmer. One day he had come home after he had been away for several weeks and told *mhama* that he had got a sugarcane farm, together with the farmhouse, that had been acquired by the government. *Mhama* had listened solemnly. I think *baba* should have written 'MRS' instead of Mr, he never works in the fields. The farm will be *mhama's* to run.

I sit staring forlornly from side to side. *Baba* does not want me to sit next to him, he says I will fall off the edge. The sun wearies on towards the hills, where it will soon disappear behind them. Vast expanses of sugar-cane, green and tall, appear on both sides of the road. We pass a farm gate, with 'R W Whyte, Farm 23' made beautifully out of metal on it. The teacher told me that 24 comes after 23, so I know the next farm will be our own. My back is now sore from sitting, but I cannot stand up or I will fall like *baba* did one day.

I know tomorrow we'll all be busy, Chido and I will be discovering our new home, *mhama* will be exploring her fields. *Baba* — he will be gallivanting, searching for the farmer who might have brewed a few drums of thick, rich *masese* ...

Maria's Independence

THE MASSES,
With clenched fists
Swept us onto the farms
There we all met. With neither hoe, tractor, plough, seed nor cow. The vast grasslands crowded our skyscraper-clouded minds and the endless *mopani* forests dimmed any memories we had of the barren sandy reserves we'd left behind. Awe filled our hearts at the sight of the many wild animals we'd heard of only in folktales or seen on the old New Geographic programmes re-run countless times by the debt-ridden state television station.

For, after many years of independent bondage, we sprang to the ancestors' beckoning to return to the land, their land, our land.

Lost through the barrel,
Won through the barrel.

Maria came from the city: the place that continues to look towards the future of our ancestors' enemies. We only knew of her after several weeks.

For when we came – even we who had arrived together – did not know the other was already there. Sometimes, we would arrive at a farm, only to be told that someone more important had already taken it, and we had to move on. And in that great confusion, we lost many a friend to the vagaries of the bush, or to wild animals whose enclosures we tore apart in our endeavours to secure a farm, even a game farm, for ourselves.

It was only when we were finally settled that someone said there was a beautiful woman in our midst. We laughed at his hallucinations. This was no place for women, we said; let alone beautiful ones.

Then we all saw her. She always wore tight pants and skimpy tops, which exposed her belly and her tummy button that seemed to point insultingly at our glazed and bloodshot eyes. No one knew what had driven her out of the glare of the city's lights onto the farms to claim a piece of our ancestral heritage for herself. She with a body so lithe, she could have been a dancer.

So, we gave her a few months to outlive the euphoria of her and our new wealth. After that she would surely move out, for she, like Martin or me, had not lighted upon the large farmhouse, or the machinery. Wasn't that, after all, what she'd hoped to acquire in the mêlée. Wasn't that what everyone wanted?

Or maybe she had people she wanted to put off a 'trail of trickery' as someone called it; someone who claimed to have seen her in the thief- and prostitute-infested avenues of Harare. Time on a farm was all the time she needed. Why else would a woman, who had a way with her eyes that left one weak-kneed, walk out on the joys of the city that never sleeps? If she did not have to escape her past, why did she join the onslaught to which only men had rushed? Or did she believe she could find better men? But we who rushed to grab were united in our poverty and of no use to a woman who looked far too complicated for our simple heads.

But even in our oneness, we were divided. For none trusted the other. Thus someone suggested that maybe she was from the opposition party, and had been sent to spy on us. But a spy of extraordinary beauty, surely not? We discussed the idea over a gallon of home-brewed *masese*, laughing and arguing about who would be able to tame her.

One man told us to let her be. 'She's more cunning than all your asses put together,' he said. 'She's too much for a woman.'

Yes, she was wild, that Maria. She would dance the *kongonya* with such gyrating movements that surely the ancestors turned in their graves and cursed the day they let the enemy bring his gramophones to the growth-points. Who could not notice the way her eyes rolled as if looking for prey while she sang the old liberation songs?

For on the farms we had rekindled the old spirits. We started holding all night *pungwes*, as in the liberation struggle. This was the third revolution and had to be treated as such if we were to fully understand what it was all about. For there were some who only understood what they'd involved themselves in after more than three months on the farms.

And when she was tired from dancing, Maria would leap into the lap of any man who happened to be sitting down. So, we took it in turns to receive the dancing goddess of the farms. When Martin's chance came, she jumped onto his lap like one possessed and threw her arms around his neck. He was about to warmly reciprocate when she shouted: 'You, get your hands off me!' And we thought the drums had fallen silent, so loud was her voice.

But Martin still told her that he really cared for her. And, with her hands still round his neck, she protested, 'Go to hell!' in a voice that almost drowned out the singers. No one ever went further than Martin; no man into whose lap she jumped every *pungwe*.

'I will tame you, one day.' Martin whispered in her ear.

'Try.' She retorted, returning to the centre of the circle.

She was untameable.

Still Maria was a woman, and the envy of many more. She would balance a twenty-litre tin of water on her head and with the grace of a lioness walk all three kilometres from the river. Maria! You had to see her heavy-laden hips swaying to and fro … You had just to walk behind her.

And she had many unknown disciples. Men followed her everywhere. Some had left their wives behind either in the cities or the sandy reserves, unsure of when someone with more power would come to chase them off the land and tell them to look for more unclaimed land. Even the men who could turn to their wives' shrivelled bosoms at the end of each hard day longed first for Maria.

'You know Martin,' Maria told him one day, 'I no longer bathe in the river because you men will follow me!' He cursed under his breath for today it was his turn to follow her to the river. But he managed to laugh and told her that she was a naughty girl and that if she didn't bath everyone would know it.

As time passed, people began to falter. The farms were not the paradise we'd thought them to be. There were no schools or clinics. We had neither the strength of our ancestors nor the machinery of our ancestors' enemies. What had once been there had been long stolen. We blistered our hands cutting down trees and tilling the soil but no rains came to quench our thirst or to water the maize.

Even the animals that had kept us clinging on disappeared one by one. Those who now found game and firewood scarce simply moved deeper into the farmlands where they remained in abundance, or did until we arrived. We had unknowingly become the bad custodians of our ancestors' wealth.

'I will miss you,' she said when Martin finally left to become an agricultural extension worker, 'but you're timid. You won't tame anything.' He smiled and told her she was a stubborn girl.

Then one day, not so long ago, Martin rode to her farm on his government-issued motorbike. Everyone else had left but Maria remained employing her own workers. He travelled through acres of maize before he reached the farmhouse. She jumped into his lap the moment she saw him, and threw her arms around his neck.

'Don't you dare,' she responded when he wanted to reciprocate by putting his gloved hands around her waist. She still wore tight pants and tops that left her belly button sticking out, as if pointedly insulting your stare. Still Martin wound his hands around her waist and told her he would be timid no more.

She tipped her head, laughed and said, 'Who's tamed who now?'

He knew she'd won. Now he goes to her farm every weekend when he does not have duties on other farms where the owners are still learning to farm years after they took over the land. Sometimes he meets her at the Revolutionary Council's organised *pungwes* and when she is tired of dancing the *kongonya* she jumps into no other man's lap except his.

The Travelling Preacher

THE PREACHER STOOD SWEATING BY THE makeshift pulpit, listening to the verses being read. Occasionally he wiped his face and nodded his head; it was then that people saw his tears.

It was always this way. Sobs would follow. Each woman would look at the man of God, then at their neighbour, and break down, sobbing. Just like that. It was tough. The children, who always sat in the front pews, would hear the sobs behind them. Nudging each other in the ribs, they would say, 'See, my *mhama* is crying.'

'And mine too,' each would respond. Then they too would also wail. And the church would fill with the sound of sobbing. And wailing. And muffled tears. Effortlessly. Just like that.

And the bible-reader would stop reading, and place the Bible on the pulpit, weeping silently, then sobbing like the women, and finally wailing like the children. Then the preacher would wipe away his tears and his sweat, and kneel down to pray, silently at first. But, when he was about to finish, he would call out in a booming voice, 'Forgive these people, Father, for they know not what they do.'

Then he would fall silent, waiting for the sobs to die down. And the women would also fall silent, just like that. But the children would continue wailing. They couldn't shut up, just like that. So, someone would sh-h-h-h, sh-h-h-the children, usually the bible-reader, for he still taught at the village crèche. Then all the children would hush, just like that. And the preacher would say, 'Bless those that empty their pockets for your work, Father. Ameeni. Ameeeni.'

Then the bible-reader would stand up and collect two deep metal dishes.

8

And Amai Piki would stand up to sing the giving song. She was big, with a large bosom and a large bottom. And how well she sang, swaying her bosom left and right, as if she was at the beerhall.

And the preacher would peep at Mai Piki through half-closed eyes over his square-rimmed spectacles, his balding head shining with sweat as metaphorically he drooled. Then the bible-reader-turned-money-collector would pass in front of him and blur his vision. And for a time, all he would see were the man's spindly arms and legs and he would curse under his breath, just like that. Then the bible-reader would move and Amai Piki would once more come into view, and the preacher would think, 'She should be able to read, I will invite her to evening classes'.

The new baas just came like that. Took away the farm and everything from Baas Tiki and never returned. The preacher also came, just like that. He appeared at the centre of the farm compound dressed in a black shirt with a white collar, black trousers, black shoes and a black jacket. All new. Very new. The large black bags he held in each hand were also new. The sun was high in the sky and very hot, and the men wouldn't have been at the beerhall if it hadn't been a Saturday, and if the farm had still belonged to the *murungu. But the new baas was always away.*

The farm village was just like any other farm compound with a road that passed through it towards the big farmhouse at the other end of the farm. Most houses were thatched. So was the church. But the beerhall and the foreman's house had corrugated roofs. And the new baas said he would corrugate all the houses. And the preacher approached the first child he saw and said, 'Child, can you show me the house of God?'

The farmhouse had everything. Murungu did not take anything when they told him to leave. The new baas then said everything was his. The child pointed at a building far away from the farmhouse. So, the preacher found his way to the house of God: an old thatched building, with no windowpanes, no door, no benches, no pulpit. Its walls had seen a lot. Its floors had felt a lot. The roof leaked when it rained, provided sunshine on clear days and dust on windy August days. Lovers entered on moony nights, and gamblers did so on Sundays. But the child had never seen a goat-faced man of God before, and choked on his laughter as he told him the way.

Three children followed him. The one that seemed to be the eldest held a bucket with a pot handle sticking out of it. A girl held the hand of the youngest, almost dragging him behind her, as they walked behind their father. She raised a fist at the child who had shown them on their way, and he looked away, afraid. So, before they reached the church at the other end of the village, all the women knew a preacherman had arrived. And they all felt pity for him because he had three children to look after and no house to sleep in. And no wife.

He threw his bags beside the old building, looked inside and cursed under his breath. He would have retched if he'd eaten. Instead, he said, 'They have turned my Father's house into a marketplace,

a gambler's haven,

an adulterer's paradise, and

the excretor's latrine.'

And he opened one bag, took out a grass broom, threw it at the girl and rasped, 'You know what to do when a place is dirty, don't you?' And to the boy he said, 'First, take out my Bible, then cook for the children.' So, the girl swept the floor and the boy gave his father the great book and went in search of water. The youngest, hungry and tired, slept beside the bags. And the preacher went away. *Just as the new baas had gone away, after he had taken the farm, and given his orders to his workers. They had to farm.*

They sold sadza and beef stew and pork stew and chicken stew at the compound beerhall. The woman cooked well. And the food smelled so well that his nose took him there.

He took out a new leather wallet, selected a few notes, and bought himself a large plate of sadza. 'With pork stew or beef stew or chicken stew?' the cooking woman asked in a sweet voice. The preacher shook his head vehemently and answered, 'Pork is unclean. Very, very unclean. And I don't like beef.' Vegetables came with every plate. So the man ate sadza with chicken stew and drank Coca Cola.

Amai Piki was at the back of the beerhall among the bushes where everyone peed. Foromani Jokoniya had once gone further under one of the bushes and his *murungu* baas had flogged the hell out of him or so Jokoniya had said. Flogged him – beard, bald-head and all – in front of his wife, children, *vakuwasha* and *varoora*; though why he would want to boast of being flogged for being dirty behind the beerhall no one knew until Jokoniya explained that *that was why the new black baas took the farm away from Baas Tiki. The new baas had fought in the war of liberation.*

10

Amai Piki had Baba Nina's hands, nose, eyes, ears, mouth and head in her big bosom. And she was giggling to herself. And Baba Nina was cursing and mumbling and saying that it should have been very, very dark. And Amai Piki giggled and said, 'Quick. Quick. Hurry up. You don't want to lose time talking do you. Hi, hi, hi.'

But Baba Nina's time was almost up, though he wanted some more, for free. After all, he'd cycled across two farms to the beerhall and Mai Piki. But at that moment, she heard the preacher and froze. Baba Nina cursed as he felt her bosom go limp in his hands. The preacher's voice was like one calling in the wilderness; calling on all to repent of their sinful ways. And, Mai Piki fastened her bra and buttoned her blouse and left Baba Nina cursing.

And the preacher preached, occasionally wiping sweat from his face. And the barman wept. So did Amai Piki and the cooking lady and all the men. And they all confessed their sins. Right there in the beerhall – the devil's sitting room. And he wrote their names in his little black book of life and urged them to come to church. And afterwards he went home, found the building swept and the floors scrubbed and the children fed.

And that night the jukebox lay still. Quiet. And no one giggled behind the beerhall. So Baba Nina confessed to Amai Nina about his philandering ways. And no one stank of opaque beer in bed. Then they talked, husbands and wives, in low hushed tones, about the new preacher and prayed the new baas would come before the rains began, until they wearily and soberly slipped into sleep.

And on Sunday church was full. Men sat on one side and women on the other. And the children sat at the front. And the preaching began, the new man in his new clothes standing by the makeshift altar with the bible-reader, the barman beside him thumbing through the pages of the Holy Book. Unused to it, he took years to find Genesis 1 verse 1 and kept looking for the New Testament in the books of Judges or Chronicles. *And someone said the new baas did not know how to farm so he had gone to school to learn how to farm. And they all knew it would take him three years to learn.* So the silent tears began. And so did the sobs of the women. And the wailing of the children. The money dishes followed.

But the men, so unused to crying and staying sober and paying tithes began to falter along the way. And they made their exodus back to Egypt. And the jukebox began to sound again, very quietly at first and later raucous above the singing voices in the church until no man remained. But there was no giggling behind the beerhall. *And the men spent all their days there. No one went to the fields. And there was no pay.* So Baba Nina had to content himself with the bosom of his wife – shrivelled by nine suckling mouths. He would sit over his calabash of *masese* and think of all the other women in this compound, in his own compound and the two compounds he passed on his way to the beerhall. All women except his own Amai Nina and say to himself, 'Oh that one has firm rounded ones. Amai Piki's breasts are just like watermelons.' So, he envied the preacher and sometimes he did not go to the beerhall.

And the preacher preached and taught Amai Piki to read and write. And she giggled a great deal, sobbed with the other women, and stood up to sing the giving song. Her hips swayed to and fro and her bosom lifted up and down, left and right. And the preacher knelt down and prayed, silently at first, but when he was about to finish, he would boom, 'Father, forgive them, for they know not what they do.'

And one day, not a year after his arrival in the village, Amai Piki took him aside after church and spoke to him. 'It seems I will never be able to learn to read and write.' She paused and breathing in deeply, continued, 'I knew I should never have given you my bosom when it was very, very dark.' He took out his handkerchief and wiped the sweat off his face, then turning to observe if there were any women nearby, he whispered, 'Just don't tell anybody about it will you, and we will see what we can do.' So, he left her, promising to be back within a week.

The rains came a long time ago. But the new baas had not finished learning how to farm. So, he had not brought any seed, or fertiliser. And the fields were not tilled. The tractors, abused, were dead. The government's tractors were still a long time away, and there was no maize in the fields. And no tobacco. Likewise, a year passed and the preacher had not returned. His children stayed with Amai Piki and went to the village school.

There was a lot of giggling behind the beerhall again, and Baba Nina cried, laughed, cursed and swore that there was nothing better than a nursing woman's bosom. And every night Amai Piki went home to suckle her baby. But she would never again give anyone her bosom when it was dark.

Specialisation

One man straightens the wire, another puts the head while another sharp-
ens the tip. In this way all men make more pins than they would if each was
to make the whole pin.
Adam Smith

SUDDENLY, EVERYTHING SEEMED TO HAVE gone wrong; but no one could tell what the cause was nor what had really happened. We sat down – Chimoto, Baba Nina and I – and in hushed tones discussed what might have occurred. But exactly five hours and two gallons of thick home-brewed opaque beer later, we'd only succeeded in getting ourselves numbly drunk and raising our voices to height-of-hot-summer cicada highs. We could have gone on. But Mhama Nina came into the study crying and saying that she couldn't stand men that knew how to do nothing except drink and argue. Why didn't we ever think of consulting the spirit medium, after all?

It was hot and a Saturday when we all crammed into the 4 x 4 single-cab truck that we had taken over along with the farm and all the other equipment. We could have gone on a Sunday, but I'd said that I would never dare insult God. Baba Nina had been the white man's driver and he still drove the truck, though I was unsure of whether it was for himself, Chimoto or me. Baba Nina had grasped specialisation with gusto and had undertaken to master the art himself. Every morning he woke up to the sound of the first singing bird. He washed the car spotlessly clean, and checked the oil and the fuel gauge. By kicking each tyre with his booted feet, he could tell which one needed more pressure, so that he could take the pump and do just that. His ritual took him until about tea-time, though tea was now rather scarce because of the countrywide sugar shortages.

Afterwards, he checked on the tractors, all three of them. He cursed and ranted every time Chimoto brought back a tractor covered in dust, mud and grime. 'Can't you even plough without muddying her up? Look at yourself,' Baba Nina would size Chimoto up and down, 'you're as dirty as the plough itself. You even leave mud on the seat!' He would pause and then turn to me. 'How can specialisation ever work if we keep frustrating each other's efforts? I'm a driver, a vehicle engineer, not a cleaner!'

I'd decided to sit next to the window where the rushing wind would cool my face and I could gaze at the vast expanses of repossessed land without straining my neck. Here and there fences that once restricted wild animals and cattle from moving onto the tarred road lay rotting on the ground or had been completely removed. It had been a rush, just like the gold rush. Everyone had wanted to take the closest entry into and onto the farms to grab the juiciest piece of ancestral soil they could find. No one had thought about tomorrow, life after the rush. The hunger had been too great and finding gates was just a waste of time.

Everywhere the land now lay bare and black, the skeletons of charred trees standing where forests had not yet been cleared. Almost everyone burnt the grass when they thought they had seen the first signs of rain. Traditional habits die hard, even when you haven't tilled for a century. The whole countryside had caught fire but no rain had followed. Not then; not now. But we could never be charged with destroying the forests with fire – it was a cultural practice. And there had always been grass-burning even before we took over the farms. It was only that now nature had decided to show us her harsher side and, of course, we had not had time to repair the fireguards, a colonial institution.

'Stop here, Chimoto,' commanded Baba Nina. We had passed the turn-off to the main road. The spirit medium's hut stood alone in the mountains, on a plateau where mermaids were said to be heard singing each morning at a spring well. Baba Nina braked hard, reversed and got onto the faint track. He manoeuvred the truck among the stones and burnt tree stumps. This way we could only take the car as far as the foot of the mountain. We got out and trudged towards the hidden hut. I felt tired and thirsty from the heat, and looking at Chimoto and Baba Nina, I knew they felt the same. 'Do you think we will find the spring with water in this drought?' I asked, breaking the silence that enveloped us.

'Shh,' Chimoto and Baba Nina said at the same time. I kept quiet, not wanting to ask why I had to shut up. Each of us walked differently. It was our specialisation. Walking. Most people said that I wobbled lazily. They said it was because of the books I'd taken to swallowing since an early age. Baba Nina walked with short brisk steps. But Chimoto had an air about him. He walked with the gaiety of all those who have ever fought in a war, whether in defeat or in victory. One need not search far for people of Chimoto's walking specialisation. They prided themselves as the country's liberators, though during the guerilla war they'd been called terrorists by Ian Smith's government or *vanamukoma* by the fearful majority in the barren sandy reserves.

And as a relic of the war, just as some wear the *légion d'honneur* or other war memorabilia, Chimoto carried a limp in the left leg where he said a bullet had entered but not come out. The limp, however, only became visible to those who didn't know him when he was angry, which was often, and when they were at a meeting for the war veterans. There was money from government for those who were injured during the struggle. It was he, Chimoto, after one of their so many meetings about this or that money who had come to tell us how absurd he thought it was that twenty years after independence, we still had not got that for which we had shed our blood.

So all we had needed to do was to wait for Baas Kisi to go to the city, as he always did every Friday, and then telephone him and say, 'You white kaffir, don't bother showing your nigger farse here because we will do your ace meat meat with a shap panga. The farm and everything on it is now ours. We, the soverin sons of the soil.' Chimoto had written down the statement so that I would not forget a word he wanted said. I told him that farse should be face and that ace had to be arse and that there was nothing like a white kaffir or white nigger but he wouldn't listen. Men of his specialisation, the country's war heroes, wouldn't listen to anyone. They knew it all and being our MPs, and old men, they spent most of their time arguing with the opposition, which only had toddlers and men with no liberation war history (except that of having been sell-outs) in parliament. I could have made him do the calling himself if he knew sufficient English and if he didn't keep on saying tell Baas Kisi this or tell Baas Kisi that.

He had been the white man's tractor driver and he still drove the tractors now though I was unsure of whether it was for Baba Nina, himself or me.

That was his other specialisation. Driving tractors. He, like Baba Nina, believed in the prowess of the Englishman's education, which was my own specialisation. I had gone all the way, according to them, though I could never tell them that half the time we had never had any lecturers since they had all gone where the fields were greener and lusher. Or we would be boycotting classes ourselves because of the inadequate government payouts to 'poor' students, or joining into any one of the unsuccessful demonstrations organised by the opposition parties. No, I could never tell them that because they believed in my ability to solve our problems.

So when I had taught them what the father of mass production had told me in those economics textbooks, they had abandoned everything they had ever known before. They had agreed that they'd never thought *mushandirapamwe* in which everyone worked together would succeed. Everyone had to do what they knew best. And that much we did. Baba Nina drove the truck. And Chimoto ploughed the fields. Mhama Nina sowed the roundnuts and groundnuts because these were a woman's crops and I sowed the maize. The children, Baba Nina's children, weeded the fields.

We reached the plateau with a final sigh of relief. Chimoto had started to complain that his leg was hurting. I did not see the spring, just as I had failed to see the farm workers in the compound the morning after we had told them we would be taking over the farm and them. We had woken up to find the whole place deserted, as if they had all been some sacred vanishing spring. Instead, I saw a spot where I thought the spring had been, nothing but a ring of stones that could only have signified a fireplace in any ordinary home. 'This is a bad omen,' Chimoto mumbled almost inaudibly.

'What?' Baba Nina asked, his face skewed into a frown. 'I said this is a bad omen,' Chimoto shouted back. I could sense that he was growing agitated. We all kept quiet and he went on talking when he realised no one was going to ask him why. 'If the spring vanishes when you arrive, the mediator will not see you. Don't you know that?'

'Can't you see it's just the drought?' I asked knowing Chimoto would never agree to any such nonsense. He just dismissed me with a flick of his hand.

The door of the lone hut that occupied the plateau stood slightly ajar. Smoke was escaping through every available escape route from the inside of the small mud, pole and grass affair. I saw the door open wider and someone, whose eyes seemed to be red, not from the smoke but from one too

16

many lungfuls of *ganja*, came out. I could tell because the weed had been popular with most students; particularly those of us who thought we had one or two choice words for the government that had failed everyone and the university administration which was nothing but a puppet of that government. It needed guts to stand and call everyone you knew that held not only your future but your life in their hands, a dog and any other such words as would make our mothers shameful of having borne us, if they ever heard that we'd spoken them. The *ganja* gave us all the blindness we needed to face our adversaries head-on, even when they came in armoured cars.

Despite those bloodshot eyes everything about the man suggested that he'd mastered the art of indifference. Maybe that was his specialisation. I could tell he had seen others like us. Hypocrites who came to visit the medium when they thought no one would ever hear about it. But despite his indifference, the man was young and extremely ugly. I could hear Baba Nina smothering a bout of laughter. I nudged him in the ribs and whispered, 'Don't you dare.' The man said 'Hi,' in English, but kept his hands behind his back like a Catholic cleric at confession, as he looked dismissively at our extended hands. We looked at each other and simultaneously withdrew our hands, though not without a little shame.

And then he said, 'I am *sekuru's* assistant.' I couldn't tell whether his remark was accompanied by a grin or a sneer, but I realised that his expression had not lost its indifference. So I didn't know whether he was glad or pissed off about being the mediator's assistant. And since he was looking me in the eye as if with a faint hint of recognition, I grinned at him, almost the grin one would expect to give when caught pants down with another man, behind the church alter.

'What brings you here, *vazukuru?*' he said, abandoning the Englishman's language, as if thinking pained him. I could almost forgive him. After all, his job was not to think but merely translate the unintelligible words of those above as the medium roared them out.

Chimoto looked at Baba Nina. Baba Nina looked at me and I could feel the intensity of his eyes, as if imploring me to find a solution from the Englishman's books I had so gullibly swallowed. But I'd never been to a spirit medium before and nor would I risk annoying the ancestors in their lairs. I looked at the ground. Baba Nina did no better. Besides cleaning cars, the only other thing he knew how to do well was drinking himself stupid and making Mhama Nina pregnant. This was why she never got to do very well in her assigned specialisation, she was always either sick or heavy. By now, she was carrying their tenth child. So, Chimoto had to speak for us. 'We want to see *sekuru*.' The assistant looked at Chimoto with indifference. Finally he spoke, the words coming out as if they had been fired from a machine gun. 'Everyone comes here to see *sekuru*. Everyone. Just say why you have come.'

'It's our farm. And it is dying.' Chimoto's voice had lost all its bravado. It was not the voice I heard when he spoke at rallies condemning anyone who opposed the government. This was the other thing I could never tell them. That we had supported the opposition parties and sacrificed our lives when we joined in their planned demonstrations. Even the teargas we had begun to call UBA perfume (which simply meant perfume for the university bachelors associates) and the bullets did not scare us at all. His voice quavered as if he would break down any minute and start to cry.

'Then go and work hard, *vazukuru*. Simply work hard.' For a moment Chimoto did not reply. He turned to look at me, for Baba Nina and I had taken a few steps back after the greeting. Realising that he could not draw anything out of our blank faces, he turned to the assistant but remained quiet.

I knew what he could have said then. That we were working extremely hard. That this year alone, he would have ploughed all the fields, that is if the diesel hadn't run out. That I was progressing very well with the planting of the maize and Mhama Nina was doing well despite her condition. Even the children had covered more than what we thought they could. It was only the rains that were letting us down, the ancestors who were refusing to let the heavens open up. He could even have told the assistant what I had taught them all those nights in our study -- the study full of the books Baas Kisi had left behind. He could have told him everything, but he chose silence.

We did not talk as we walked back to the car. Somehow I remembered hearing the medium's assistant saying that we couldn't talk to the medium for one or another reason. But it had nothing to do with a spring that had vanished nor did it have anything to do with the medium having gone to a government function. Because after all these years, our war heroes had suddenly remembered that they still needed the ancestors' specialist protection against their enemies (an opposition that wanted to get all of them out of power, not the former white colonists). He stated it all in that indifferent staccato voice of his and hadn't even bothered to reply when I thought I heard Chimoto inquiring when we could come back.

Even then, I was doubtful whether I would traverse this road again, but maybe I would, not to see the medium, but his assistant because I thought that I had once seen him at university. Then he'd seemed an enthusiastic student with a good future in the specialist field of psychology, if there were any jobs for him when he graduated. The money we'd intended to give *sekuru* lay heavy in my pocket, and I ran back to where the spring ought to have been and placed it there. Taking one final look before I descended the mountain, I saw him pick it up, count it and shout 'AHOY', which was the UBA salute, in a tone that had no indifference at all. In fact it contained all the triumph that we felt at Hunger Square after another successful demolition of our halls of residence, complaining of poor living conditions.

I remembered that we – Chimoto, Baba Nina and I – had forgotten to find someone who knew about irrigation. Someone who would wake up each morning with the same gusto as we did to do what they had to do. Our dam was still full and the irrigation equipment was lying idle. Maybe specialisation could work after all, if only we could find someone with the right skills to join us.

Having my Way

IT WAS IN THE TENTH MONTH OF THE SECOND year of our occupation of the farms that a very unfortunate incident happened. Tonde, whom we had always suspected of having hallucinations, raped Maria. It was regrettable. He made it worse by insisting that he knew Maria and that they'd once been married, and by not escaping when he might have done. The justice of the farms was instant. The liberation war creed reigned – we refused to recognise the slow colonial justice system adopted by our government. We beat up thieves, chased out adulterers and severely beat, or killed, suspected sell-outs of the revolution. Thus an emergency *pungwe* meeting was convened in the tractor-shed at Chimoto's farm. It was a strange meeting because Maria, the queen of *kongonya*, simply sat in a folding chair, her head held high in defiance of the established order of manhood and stared Tonde straight in the face. But everyone else sang revolutionary songs, which ignited the spirit of the liberation struggle. Our being on the farms was a continuation of that struggle. We all knew that. We'd been told often enough.

What made the case more unfortunate were at least two additional facts. There had never been a reported case of rape before, or at least one so zealously followed through. All previous cases having been treated as essential to the revolutionary egos – a necessary and inevitable statement of our independence. However, when Tonde used this rationale, Maria shot him down with the speed of an AK-47.

It must also be remembered that Tonde was a senior member of the Revolutionary Council headed by the commander, Chimoto, and the council ruled supreme. It decided who got what and who didn't on the farms that fell under its jurisdiction. It determined who was a patriot, and who furthered the ways of the enemy. Indeed, it pronounced on all the issues peculiar to any revolution. It must be noted that in the early days of the land revolution, it was only greedy but absent politicians, the uneducated and unemployed, and the war veterans (to spite their old white enemies) who found themselves taking over farms. This made me the only recognised member of the council who had gullibly devoured the colonialists' education, so I acted as secretary, recording the proceedings verbatim with an old typewriter that we had salvaged from Baba Nina's house.

Tonde began his defence, staring into empty space, talking as if he was addressing an imaginary being. He could as well have been possessed for he seemed to go into a trance before speaking in a different voice.

Do you remember Peter, who used to live next door to us in Mucheke, that old suburb in Masvingo? But you would never call that next door would you? The house was just one big room divided by thin sheets into three separate areas for three families — two being childless couples. Peter was the one who was as dark as ebony, though he had a wife who was darker still.

Maria raised her hands, laughing and protesting the start of Tonde's defence. Chimoto, already incensed by her insistence on sitting in a chair, shut her up with a sneer. Tonde continued oblivious of the interruption.

Why are you laughing? You are naughty. I know that you want to tell me that you remember his wife who shouted and wept every night when they made love. You could be forgiven for thinking that Peter was using a whip. And how they loved to do it with the lights on and we would watch them through the thin sheets like some big-screen pornographic movie.

But I know you may want to ask me what Peter and his sex-hungry wife have to do with Tinashe. I'm sorry, my dear, but sometimes my mind wanders, and I forget what it is I should be saying.

A man, in the crowd laughed but finding himself alone in his response, he shut up, coughing uneasily as if his laugh had been an aberration.

Tinashe lived behind our own section of the curtain-partitioned room. Unlike Peter, you could never hear a sound when he and his wife steamed it off. Sometimes when you and I lay on my bed, which covered four-fifths of the room, we would ask each other whether the couple behind us ever actually did it at all.

Sometimes I would lie awake for whole nights, peeping through the cur-

21

tain. I never saw any upheaving of blankets. I felt pity for his wife work-ing through her chores every morning with that same gloomy look on her face.

Tonde paused, as if for effect.

Did you know that Tinashe and his wife were excommunicated when they fell in love? They were at the same mission before they moved to the city. It was silly of them you know. They'd been ordained, both of them, priest and nun, and each knew they were not supposed to fall in love with earthly beings.

Do you remember that we used to share the bathroom, which still had a squatting toilet all these years after independence? No. Don't tell me to leave politics alone as you always did in those days when I was retrenched during ESAP.

'Don't talk politics, Cde Tonde.' Chimoto growled uneasily. Tonde turned around and seemed to be looking at Chimoto but the strange trance-like look on his face didn't alter.

One day, Tinashe came into the bathroom when I was there. He'd seen me enter and knocked lightly on the ramshackle door but didn't wait for my reply before he barged in. I even messed my trousers as I hurriedly tried to cover my nakedness. I'd thought it might be Peter's wife for she was in the habit of following me to the bathroom.

He paused as if waiting for a response but Maria kept quiet, her face wore a bored expression as if she was tired of the farce.

I never told you about this, of course. You're crazy. Would I tell you that she never cried out when I took her? I wondered what it was that Peter did that made her weep so.

Tinashe closed the door behind him and stood there watching me. I could see that it had nothing to do with him being in a rush to use the hole, for he was very calm. He looked me down from head to toe as if it was the first time he'd seen me. Now, my dear, I can tell you I felt very un-comfortable.

I buttoned my trousers without looking at his face then I turned to leave but he remained in the doorway. So, I too just stood there waiting for his next move. We both stood there for what seemed like hours, him looking at me and me staring at the ground. The floor was dirty, very dirty.

I could not that day determine the thickness of the grime though I had time to do so. I could not concentrate as I was so aware of the man standing there, enjoying this unusual encounter. If it had been Peter, I would have said a prayer to those above asking for protection, but with this man, I didn't know what to do. I knew of no wrong I had done him.

'Go on,' Maria shouted irritated.

At last, I spoke. I knew that Tinashe was rarely one to start or take part in a conversation on any issue. Even when we men sometimes sat outside in the sunshine talking about football or politics, Tinashe would only stare forlornly into space seemingly oblivious of what we were saying.

I did not know whether to address this man rudely or politely – rudely because he had greatly inconvenienced me or politely because I feared for his reaction. The room was too small and he stood at the only exit.

'What is it, Moyo' I asked trying to sound nonchalant.

For a long moment he did not respond and then he only said, 'I know…'

'You know what?'

'Don't get angry.' He said calmly. 'We can work this out. I know about you and Peter's wife, but I won't tell him if you agree to my conditions.'

'So you agreed?' Maria asked sarcastically.

You know I wouldn't have agreed, though you said it would have been easier that way. But you were wrong. Even if I'd needed the money he offered, he asked too much for it. I know you'd told me you would leave me if I didn't get a job. That was OK with me: I was tired of your nagging. I wished you were more like Tinashe's wife, who was deprived of both money and sexual pleasure, but still went about her duties like a woman should, quietly and obediently. Besides, could I ever live with the shame of submitting to another man?

Did you really know Tinashe? The humble, former man of God, who lived with his wife in the room behind our own. Remember how we said that it was silly of the church leaders to fire a man so clearly not of this world. Weren't those sexless nights clear testimony of that? You thought you knew him well, didn't you? Well, you didn't know him at all!

I'd never known Tinashe to be violent but he took a knife out of his pocket. I studied the weapon carefully. It was an okapi whose blade could be drawn back into the handle. It looked very sharp. If he used it on me, I would die the way my grandfather died, with a knife in his gut. Tinashe was turning the knife slowly in his hands, knowing the effect it was having on me, but never taking his eyes off my face.

Perhaps memories of my grandfather had sapped my strength but I let him take me like a beast, his body heaving against mine. The force of his penetration was intense, and I gave a cry of pain. I could feel blood trickling off my bruised anus while his contented grunts bruised my ears. When he finally pulled himself away, I could feel warm tears coursing down my cheeks. I did not open my eyes to see what he would do next. But he just closed the door softly behind him and I remained kneeling where I was.

Tears were streaming down Tonde's face. I looked at Maria and saw that her own expression had softened.

Afterwards, I could never bring myself to look into the eyes of this man whom, I subsequently discovered, had not been expelled from the church for falling in love but for paedophilia and sodomy. I'd always felt he'd been unjustly treated. Wasn't every man free to choose whom they wanted to share their bed with? I'd never imagined that under that humble demeanour lay a demon that would not only blackmail, but could kill to get what he wanted. A man who had tricked a devout young nun in to marriage and the appearance of normality, promising her a family that he knew he would never give her.

Later it dawned on me that he'd been at it with Peter, which was why they sometimes took a bath together. But how he got Peter to submit to him, that I do not know.

Something in Peter died. His wife did not scream or groan with pleasure anymore, and she began to follow me into the bathroom at night. But I could never satisfy her. Finally, she left him, and it was not many days afterwards that he moved onto the streets.

I feared the same for myself. Some days I gave myself to him, sometimes even on my own bed, sometimes even with pleasure. Sometimes he played with his knife, while he entered me. That was Tinashe playing with love, with submission, with fear, pretending that all was OK between us.

When you left me, I knew you had found someone else. I could hardly blame you. I was not the husband I'd once been. But it was a nail in my coffin. I feared that I too would follow Peter onto the streets.

That was why you saw me at your door on that cold winter's day a year later. Even after I'd sworn that I would never beg you to return. But to me *it did not matter any more. I begged you to let me in being your first 'husband'. You knew it was only normal that I do that.*

But you said that you were not you. How could you? You insisted that you did not know Tinashe. You would have understood why I acted the way I did, if you had chosen to remember him. I had to convince myself that nothing in me had died, that I was still a man after all these nights with Tinashe on top of me.

Tonde turned to the council and for the first time started addressing something we could all see.

But Maria would not take me freely as she'd done before – she kept insisting that she wasn't the person I'd once known, so how could she accept me as her husband?

He turned again and this time looked squarely at Maria and then he knelt before her. The revolutionary guard moved to drag him away but Maria motioned for him to leave Tonde alone. A young unkempt youth with a long hippo-hide sjambok strapped to his back like a gun looked at Chimoto unsure of what to do but received the same signal.

I had to force myself on you. I'm sorry I didn't hear that your moaning was different. Maybe you've changed, maybe you no longer remember the past. Still it was the same, almost the same, to me. You are still my Maria who used to wear tight pants, and tops that left your belly button sticking out.

I wish you would forgive me just as I have taught myself to forgive Tinashe. Did you know that he lived with an abusive uncle from the age of five. He only managed to get away when he was nineteen and was accepted at the seminary? Peter's wife told you that. Remember?

Maria slowly shook her head.

You say you didn't know that!?

Tonde looked perplexed and fell silent for a moment before he said, 'Then you probably never knew either Tinashe or me?'

He sank down to the ground at Maria's feet I set the typewriter down, and looked at Maria whose face was wet with fresh tears. She had come determined to send Tonde down, she had told me herself earlier, but now …

Everyone watched somberly, neither ready to pick up sticks to beat him up nor prepared to have him forgiven. They awaited the Council's decision.

But no one seemed prepared to pass a judgement. Chimoto said that we would meet again the following day. That day never came for we woke up to find Tonde gone and Maria told the revolutionary guards not to bother searching for him.

The Second Trek – Going Home

I JUMP OFF THE BIG BED. *Mhama* always tells me that one day I will break my legs. I wonder if the *murungu's* children didn't jump like me. (I have their photographs under my mattress. I stole them from the pile *baba* wanted to burn.) Besides, I can't take my time because Chido is wailing. I have to run and tell her to keep quiet before *mhama* comes and tells her to shut up. She isn't a baby any more, but she won't stop crying. She even cries before anyone has hit her; *mhama* didn't even cry when *baba* hit her with his hoe handle.

Now she can't weed the fields any more. Only *sekuru* works quietly among the sugar-cane. Sometimes I go with him. There is no school here. There are no other children. They all went away with their parents when *baba* couldn't pay them. Only *sekuru* didn't go. I asked him why and he said that he had nowhere to go. He looked away when he said this and I thought he would cry. His voice was very funny. *Mhama* says he is from a faraway country called Malawi, that's why he speaks like that. I asked him why he didn't get his own farm like *baba*. He did not reply. He just put his hoe down on a pile of dried sugar-cane.

It's last year's sugar-cane. We harvested it when we arrived. *Mhama* has forgotten the old priest now. She doesn't go to church any more. No one tells her to reap only where she sowed. There are piles and piles of sugar-cane. The whole farm is full of it because *baba* couldn't find a tractor to take it to the mill. He says *murungu* should have left the tractors. I wonder why he left everything else. Even the dead *mesidhisi-bhenzi*. That's what baba said it's called, the car under the big mango tree next to our scotch cart. *Baba* says everything is now ours, so we won't need a rickety, wobbly scotch cart any more. Everything belongs to us.

I go through the sitting room. *Mhama* has moved the sofa so as to keep the door open. It still doesn't close or open properly after *baba* broke it to let us in when we arrived. There's a man sitting on the leather sofa that *baba* always sits on. I don't know when he arrived. He's staring blankly at the TV. It's not on. It hasn't been switched on for a long time now, like the stove and the thing that goes in hoo-hoo-hoo – sucking in all dirt from the carpet. Mhama knows about all these things. She once worked for a *murungu*. But it's been a long time since the man in the van came to switch off the electricity.

I don't have to go to Chido's room any more. She is quiet now. *Mhama* is looking at the man. She raises her head to look at me and then looks down. There are tears in her eyes. Once I asked *sekuru* why Mhama never cries. I know I don't cry because I'm a man. *Baba* said only women and girls should cry. One day he beat me up for crying when I fell off the scotch cart. He never beats Chido. *Sekuru* said older people cry only when something very bad has happened.

Baba has not been home for a week now. *Mhama* once said that beer will be his death. So maybe he has finally got himself killed. Is that why she's crying? Now maybe she can go and fight *sekuru*. With the plaster cast on her left hand, I know she can beat him. She blames him for all our misfortunes. She says it's because he liked *murungu* too much that he doesn't want us to become rich and is using medicine to make our sugar-cane fail to grow. She told me that she once caught him walking naked in our backyard in the middle of the night. I wondered where she was going because her own room doesn't face that way. Besides we don't go outside to take a wee in the night, there is a little toilet in the house with a stool stronger than *baba's* rotten stool.

The man looks at me. He stands up to go. He takes his hat, which I had not seen from where I stand, and perches it on his head. It has a star stuck on its front. He takes one more look at *mhama* and after scanning the whole room with squinted eyes, makes for the door. He stands there for a moment and tells her to be ready tomorrow morning. *Mhama* doesn't say anything. I want to run after him and ask him why he has come. But *mhama* won't let me. Her eyes tell me I am in trouble for eavesdropping. I know she can still beat us even with the plaster on her hand.

I know *sekuru* is in the fields. Maybe the man went to him as well. I have to go and talk to him. Though it is still early in the morning, the sun is very hot. It hasn't rained for a long time now. The soil is parched. Even in the sugar-cane fields there are big cracks in the ground. If only *baba* had come home with the money from selling the ox and the cow. The calf was stolen. We all grieved for it – *mhama*, Chido and I – but not *baba*. If we had money, maybe the engines would now be working and we would have enough water to irrigate the fields. There might even be fertiliser. That's what *sekuru* told me the crops needed to grow.

Sekuru is working in the sun. I look at him for a while. He is working harder than he ever does. Sweat trickles down his head and his thin shirt is already wet. He does not stop to look at me even when I cough to make him notice I have arrived. He has an opaque beer container next to him. I never knew that he drank beer when he was working. But who brought him the beer?

I tell him that *mhama* has been crying. He looks at me scornfully. He does not say anything. I watch him as he goes on working furiously. He is repairing the canal, putting the loose blocks in order. Someone must have told him to do this. But it isn't mother. She hasn't come to the fields for two months now. I wonder if *baba* finally sent someone with the money from the sale of the cattle. *Sekuru* continues working. He doesn't want to listen to me.

Night comes and we wake up again in the morning. The sun is hot. *Baba* still hasn't come back. The policeman – that's what *mhama* said the man with a star on his hat is called – says *baba* will come after us when we are gone. Chido plays close to *mhama*. At first, she wouldn't get into the truck that the police brought to carry us away. But *mhama* told her it was just a bigger scotch cart, and Chido likes to play in our old scotch cart. I don't know why they brought guns and big helmets with glasses on them.

When she saw them, *mhama* left behind most of the things she had packed. *Baba* is a problem. But I know that if they come with helmets, he won't say a thing. Only *sekuru* remains on the farm now. And as we pass by the vast expanses of our stunted sugar-cane, I can see him still working, ignoring the hot sun. He does not even raise his head to look at us and he seems unperturbed by the big black *mesidhisi-bhenzi* parked beside the field. There is a man with a big stomach standing beside it. Maybe if *baba* worked hard he would also have a stomach like that.

We pass by the farm gate. The driver does not stop. I wanted to take the metal board with 'Mr B J Magudu, Black Commercial Farmer, Farm 24' and throw it far far far away. But we are heading for home now. I know tomorrow we will all be busy. Chido will be wailing as usual. There will be school for me. But above all, the old priest will come visiting, with some scriptures to make *mhama* cry.

Tonde's Return

MUKOMA TONDE – AS SHE HAS BEEN TAUGHT to call him, even though he is two years younger than her – stood beside the pillar supporting the sagging verandah roof of the old store. It was just where the little messenger said they would find him. She approached, unsure of whether it really was her brother after all these years.

She stopped, released the handles of the heavy barrow, and glanced about her like someone who realises they're lost. But this was her own township and she knew it well. It was only with respect to her sibling that she suddenly understands that a lot else may have been lost. She does not know him any longer.

Ignoring everyone standing beside him, she asks without preliminaries 'Where are the bags?' But if she has overcome her anxiety with quick action, her voice betrays her. He ignores the unspoken greeting, the lack of courtesy, and points towards a tree. Then, without a word walks towards it, as if expecting her to follow him. The scud in his hand seems too heavy for him, and he puts it down next to his belongings in the wheelbarrow.

And she, more out of tradition and intuition than sisterly compassion for a brother who has been away for ten years, iterates, 'How are you *mukoma*?' bending her knees and holding her hands together in one weak clap. He noticed how little she had changed, and replied that he was well and asked how she was herself. She did not respond.

Her mind is already battling with what to say next. She had wanted to run and hug him and ask a lot of questions. Why had he come back after all these years with neither wife nor children to show for his exploits in the big city? Why did he now wear dreadlocks? Why had he grown so dark, as if he'd been working on the farms or in the Hwange coal mine?

But there had been too many people at the store. They would say it was un-womanly, unAfrican, of her to show so much emotion and ask too many questions. Brothers and sisters do not have to be intimate. They only have to shake hands, like father and daughter, mother and son. That was that. No level of modernisation would change the culture of expectation regarding manners. After all, it was the people's disobedience, which had caused all the many droughts. The ancestors were angry.

Silently, she began pushing the wheelbarrow taking the foot-beaten path that led south towards their home. Her brother followed, walking with the slow, erratic steps of a child learning to walk. There was something troubling her; he could sense it in her hesitation. Remembering her attitude to men, he had not expected to find her married, but still he'd been taken aback to see her pushing the wheelbarrow. He wondered if her being still at their parents' home had anything to do with their father.

Every time the old man had become angry with Tonde, he would evoke all kinds of evil spirits on his innocent daughter, for who could risk cursing one's son, the one whom he hoped would continue the lineage, feed the tribal fire. After all, she was the eldest and surely the one who had encouraged her younger brother in his misdemeanours.

Away from the township, she felt less intimidated by the eyes of strangers. Still, communication was an effort after almost a decade of silence. But she knew she had to talk to make her brother feel welcome.

'Do you drink now?' she asked, staring at the opaque beer container.

He did not reply. She knew she should not have asked that question. It was rude. Did she not see, from his uneven steps, that he was drunk anyway? After all, dreadlocked men who came from the city always drank and smoked *mbanje*? Had Gari been any different from Tonde?

'Maybe I shouldn't have asked that,' she apologised.

'No. I don't drink. This is for father,' he replied calmly, pointing at the scud.

She thought he was lying and when she raised her eyes to his face, their eyes met. She had always been able to tell if he was being untruthful. His eyes were emotionless. Blank. But suspecting that she did not believe him, he said shrugging, 'And the dreadlocks, they're nothing. Just a hairstyle really.'

She knew it was something — to her anything was something. The dreads meant that he had not become what their parents had wanted him to be, an office worker. She determined that she would not argue with him. Not as they'd always done in the past anyway. Perhaps silence was now the best form of communication, not the noisy arguments they used to have that surprisingly always drew them closer together.

A soft breeze rose from a new direction and she felt the strong odour of his unwashed clothes. She wondered how long it was since he had bathed and why he had chosen to travel smelling as he did. It was shameful.

'When did you leave the city?' she asked him half turning her face away.

'Years back.' He replied casually, catching her off-guard. He walked mechanically as if not noticing where he was going, stumbling over small gulleys and tree stumps. He ignored her few hesitant questions as if his mind was elsewhere. She was not offended; she was beyond that. Not that she considered herself inhuman, but life had shown her enough not to be moved by trivialities such as people ignoring her presence. She hoped that one day they would communicate again, as they had done so often as children.

It surprised, even shocked, her that he'd left the city for a number of years. He'd never written to them to say he was moving on or to give them an address. Not that he was one for writing. The first and last letter they'd received had been eight years ago. She'd kept it, still in its brown envelope. It was the closest she got to him and she treasured it. Then he had written about a woman called Maria with whom he was living and how much he hoped to bring her home. They'd all waited patiently, hoping to meet this mystery woman. And when she never came, the girl came to believe that Maria had stolen her brother away from her.

But now looking at him, his clothes unwashed and his body emaciated, she wondered whether he'd been in the arms of any woman for a long time. It was clear that something more than the mysterious Maria had stolen his spirit. He seemed to have lost his soul.

As they passed Kunaka's homestead, they observed three children playing beside their sleeping grandfather. It was said that Kunaka had lost his mind. When he wasn't sleeping, he haunted the township looking for his last-born son. He never lamented the curse the gods had placed on him. Each of his four other children lay buried next to their mother.

Now even his grandchildren were dying, thin and emaciated like their parents. How could he accept that they were all dying from the same disease when he himself who had borne them did not have it? Even his wife did not have it for she had died quietly while he was out drinking, neither thin nor drained.

The girl looked at Tonde who was staring at the new mounds of earth beside Kunaka's kitchen. Three of them did not look more than a year old. Could she tell him that one of them belonged to his friend, Farai? Maybe later. Now she kept her silence and looked at the three children, who had ceased playing and were staring suspiciously at the two passers-by. She did not shout a greeting to Kunaka for she knew the old man would not reply.

They walked on in silence, each conscious of the rhythm of the other's footsteps. They had learnt all their life to look after each other and she wondered if she had somehow failed him. Ahead, a lone cicada made his mating call. Soon the sun would slide behind Nyamungwe Mountain and the whole horizon would glow a deep orange before darkness set in.

She felt that she was back at Gari's graveside and the men were taking turns to fill up the hole. She hadn't been able to wail like Gari's mother or sister for no one knew that she had loved him. It was her secret, and it stayed that way.

They reached the dry riverbed. They'd been walking slowly. Her brother looked visibly tired. Rotting trees held each other up with sinewy leafless branches over the heavily grooved path. A smell of rotting flesh filled the air. Cattle came to the river desperate for water and each day a few of them fell by the wayside: thirsty, hungry and weary from the endless quest for grass in the bone-dry land.

When her brother had left them, the river had never dried up; then it had seemed that his ideas and opinions would likewise never cease to flow. But now the river was dry and he too had changed, his soul parched, his words soundless.

They stopped on the sandy riverbed and she sat in the wheelbarrow with his meagre belongings. Tonde was sweating, the stench from his body intense. He looked at his sister, aware for the first time of his own smell, and that she was keeping her distance. He wondered if she was happy to have him come home.

'What happened to the river?' he asked, wiping away the sweat — or was it tears? — from his cheek with the back of his hand. She'd never seen him cry, not since father had told him that he was a man when he was only two years old. Sometimes she had cried for him but she didn't think this would happen again, she would cry no more. She had hardened too.

'It's the drought.'

'Where do the animals drink now?' He began digging deep into the soft white sand of the dry riverbed for some water. There was none, she knew it, but he had to discover this for himself.

'The cattle are dying,' she replied, looking at him. Can't you smell them? And look at the bones.'

Gari too had died so suddenly. No one had known of their relationship. But she and Gari had done and seen enough of each other for her to be fearful. Death was everywhere. Now she found she was even more afraid for her brother. People were dying of the disease of the cities, and he was so thin. Had he, like Gari and Kunaka's children, come home to die and to kill others. No one, not she nor Kunaka nor anyone else would ever understand how they had so wronged the gods and the ancestors.

Keeping her thoughts to herself, she told her brother that there was now a borehole seven kilometres from their village. It was the best the NGOs or the churches could offer them, in addition to their monthly ration of mealie-meal. No one died of hunger. After all meat was in abundance, wasn't it? Later, she would tell him why that was.

Machinda's bank on their side of the river was steep and slippery. When they reached the flat granite rock at the top, Tonde stopped to rest, then started to cough. It must have been the noise that alerted their mother who came running to meet them. Her lopsided church doek revealing her now grey hair. It had almost become a status symbol, this sign of age or longevity. The elders said that the young people would never live to see their own grey hair.

She threw her arms around her son's thin body and then let go, as if feeling the coldness within him. He raised his hand and took off his coloured hat in mock salutation, though avoiding her eyes.

Tears welled up in their mother's eyes. Was this the boy she had once known, the boy she had borne? Was this the boy who had allowed her to face her in-laws with some pride, after they mocked her for first giving birth to a girl? Had he not been her shield from her husband's abuses. '*Mmwanangu,*' she whispered, 'What did they do to you?' and her tears fell unchecked.

Silently, they reached home, the evening meal was ready and they ate together, Tonde picking slowly at the food that his mother had so carefully prepared. After the meal, nothing more could be said. It was dark, and the night had ears and they were evil. The morning was the time to discuss more important issues like that of the three-month-old mound of soil behind the house that Tonde had not yet seen. His father had been another who had come home to die after spending four years on the farms. They had not even known where he had been at first, giving him up for lost, only to have him brought home by three shabby young men who said they had picked him up about forty kilometres away.

Mother quietly left the fire first as if wishing her children goodnight would prompt more tears. Tomorrow she would be pushed to the clinic in the wheelbarrow. Her sugar levels and high blood pressure were bad these days. They heard her muttering, 'My God. My children, what have they done wrong? What is it, my God?'

'What is it Tonde?' she asked when mother's voice could no longer be heard. Though she had a feeling that it was that which ate up Gari and Kunaka's children; that which might one day eat her up. That which would mean they would not care for their parents' graves or see their own *imvi*.

Her brother was coughing again. When it subsided, he stood up and said, 'I think I'm dying sisi. Now let me sleep.' She heard the door of his hut close. She felt warm tears on her cheeks and for the first time since Gari's death, she let herself cry. She would sleep on his doorstep, watching over him.

Tomorrow she would teach him to live. He had to find his soul and learn to live again. But she knew that it was more than the illness, more than his life with Maria, more than a failed life in the city, more than the mysterious life he had lived afterwards that haunted him. Tonde had a story to tell and she would listen to it.

A Dream and a Guitar

KUNAKA KNEW THAT PEOPLE THOUGHT HE HAD gone mad. They whispered behind his back. He needed no words. Having chosen to live all these years as the village's outcast, he had learnt to master the language of faces and gesture. Rarely did he observe anything good.

Recently he had begun to have nightmares. They'd been prompted after VaMakei's son, Tonde, had returned home with the emptiness that all his children had brought home. Dreams he had never previously had came to haunt him in his old age. One kept repeating itself like the bioscopes beamed on school walls and in community halls in Salisbury. Night began to frighten him.

He took comfort in his guitar, but no matter what or for how long he played, eventually he needed to sleep — and to dream. Like hungry lions the nightmares pounced.

Not that he didn't know the city, he did. Whatever his parents had thought, and they had no time for a minstrel in the family, the guitar had opened doors to him. Black and white had welcomed him; making him feel at home in that impersonal city, which rarely cared for its black inhabitants. Highfields was the place he found where he could make money playing in all its beerhalls where men went to drown their anger and frustration after a hard day in the factories. But he had outgrown Highfields and gone where the masters went.

He had made money and had sent some of it home to his mother. He had even told them to buy cattle for him. Still most of his money was spent on the basics: food, clothing and sex. The sex sellers were few, but he had taken his own share without grumbling, and left enough for others so there was rarely any fighting for this scarce commodity.

Of course, he had received his own share of STDs, again without grumbling, holding his disfigured penis with a sense of accomplishment, for the bull that fights is seen by the wounds it carries. He had grown up herding cattle with other young men, where one had to bear one's scars, otherwise you would not be believed.

He remembers the first time he got a VD but could not remember which of the several women had given it to him. Not that he ever asked them their names or cared to do so. What he knew was only for the bravado of discussion with other men. Complexion, breast size, performance, amount charged. His totem, Gono, was a raging bull. He had been more than a raging bull on that occasion, and had gored three of them in just two days. VD was collateral and got himself a shot for it at the clinic. The black male nurse aide had shaken his hand and had told him where there were safer women to be had.

And the guitar had taken him there, and to many places where pleasure and not the plague would swallow one up and one could forget there was a war raging in the countryside. Queens, The Terreskane, Mushandirapamwe and other nameless bars and hotels where the white soldiers would call him 'The Guitar Terrorist' and only allow him to play after they'd searched him to be sure that he wasn't carrying any weapons. Then, after his show, taunt him to please take any one of those 'beautiful ladies' sitting there, white, and smoking cigarettes.

Although no one he knew had died of an STD, he had woken up after a solo performance at the Hotel Elizabeth with a thick head, and felt that it was time to go. He took the first bus home.

How could he now be expected to believe that the same town he had once inhabited and left unscathed was now ferociously consuming its inhabitants? Apart from the name change, how could Salisbury be any different from the Harare his own children had adventured into, returning dead or dying.

Never before had dreams frightened him. Why was it the sight of someone else's child that had evoked these nightmares? Even, as a young man, when his mother had died, she had not returned to bid him farewell as they told him would happen. Neither had his children forewarned him of their departure in his dreams.

He had always believed that to dream, or to think or talk about them is a woman's pursuit. When, all those years back, his wife had told him her dream, he had listened impatiently, strumming a tune to her words on his guitar, angry that she was keeping him from going to a beer party. He could have gone, just like that, and left her grumbling to herself, but he knew not to shut the door on her.

Not that she was a bad wife. There had never been a day when he'd had to wear torn or dirty clothes, nor was his stomach ever empty. Moreover, she gave him sons, nor did she deny him the prospects of filling his kraal with cattle, for she had given him an equal number of daughters. Eight children in all.

But even he knew that *ura mapoko hwunozvara mbava nevaroyi*, the womb is capable of carrying thieves and witches. So he had not expected too much of his children, but glad to see them grow up the envy of the village and when each had taken a bus to the city, he had let them go without happiness or sorrow. Kunaka was a realist; he knew the barren soils held no more hope for his sons or his daughters.

It now seemed a long long time ago that he had rushed out of the door the moment his wife had finished bothering him with her womanly tales – her dreams. In fact, she'd been frightened and had begged him to stay, but he had promised to return after only three or four mouthfuls. He wouldn't stay long, he'd told her, after all who didn't know that Mai Bernard's beer was always the worst brewed in all the seven villages. The only reason people kept on going to her parties was to see whether this time she had beaten her previous record for bad home brew.

Inevitably, he had stayed longer than he intended though the beer was worse than ever. They had to half-carry him to his wife's cold body just as the sun had begun to set. Everyone had felt pity for the poor woman who had died alone while her useless husband gulped down mouthfuls of bad beer. They also cursed her children who did not bother to attend their mother's graveside. Her spirit would definitely take its vengeance on them all, they said knowingly.

Thus, no one was surprised when each of his children returned home to die. Three of his daughters, skeletons all and none with a husband, came with only a bagful of clothes and two or three malnourished babies. The other one, the eldest, arrived dead, the children crammed in with their mother's stinking corpse in the police van.

And none of his children knew where the others were, expressing shock when they returned to find the others dead. Each, in their own way, seemed to have been swallowed by the city that never slept.

And each, as if feeling guilty for having thought their parents immortal, blamed him for not having told them about their mother's death. Even then, he had not been angry with any of them, but had accepted each of them and their children without asking where the fathers were or where they thought they had been all this time. Instead, he had greeted each one of them with a slaughtered goat, merriment and a song on his guitar.

He had always played for them, songs when they were born, and songs when they left. But if his playing had evoked emotion then, the guitar produced no such emotion now. They arrived, emaciated, lifeless and without humour. Each had died before the other arrived. For two years, his was the only home that saw death in the village. That was when they had said he had a *tokoloshi* to eat his own children.

He had not heeded their words. How could he blame them for misinterpreting a curse those above him had placed on him? For to do so would mean that he would be blaming those above as well and he knew well enough not to do that. Instead, he had chosen silence.

And now he waited anxiously for one of his children, the only one left. He had written a letter to his father saying that he was coming but he did not say when. He was the youngest and Kunaka had always thought him the most sensible. The letter had come months before, and he kept it tucked safely in his jacket. He had searched for clues to his son's health, but finding none, he had been hopeful, telling himself aloud that his son would return home healthy.

Every day, strumming a mellow tune on his guitar, he would wait for the bus in the township, not too far off, and when he saw no sign of his son, returned with an even merrier tune. That was when the villagers began to say that the wires were growing loose in his head. But he did not mind them because he knew they did not know about the letter from his son.

But the sight of VaMakei's son evoked all the fears he now had in his life. The boy had the same resigned look and demeanour that all his other sons had carried when they returned home to die. He had once heard that the boy had not been in Salisbury, or whatever they called it now, but to him it was all the same. He wondered if there were any towns of the new country that would not swallow its children.

For him the old country had had its own perils, like the liberation struggle and the segregation, but never did anything threaten to wipe out whole generations. Did the coming of freedom therefore mean the coming of the plague?

He waited, offering silent prayers each night. He prayed for his last-born to come home as he'd said he would. Alive. Not bedridden or in a ramshackle police coffin. On that occasion, even Kunaka had failed to recognise his own daughter, his first fruit. He had simply buried her, knowing that the plague could change people. Like all the others, she now lay beside her mother.

But now the dream gave him no rest. It was the same dream he now remembers his wife telling him all those years previously. A dream they said meant the coming of only one thing: death. It was not the fear of death that made him fear the dream. He had long become indifferent to both life and death. It was that, unlike his wife, he had no one to tell of his recurrent nightmare. The plague was robbing him of all he had to say.

He could only speak to one who would live a long time from now. Someone who would recall the dream when their own time came and tell it to others. His two grandchildren, the only ones left of the nine his daughters had brought him, were too ill and too young to be good ears. He wanted his son.

Yet, he could never bring himself to accept the nagging thought that it was not the sight of vaMakei's son but the appearance of his own son deep in the night of that same day which had triggered his nightmares. From that moment, he had felt increasingly disturbed. Finally, he too had begun to believe that he was losing his mind. Still he hoped, against all hope, that his memories and dreams were just an illusion. He had thought too hard about his son and somehow conjured up a living image of him. After all, he knew the ways of magic having once played the accompanying guitar music to a Malawian magician's show and seen all sorts of creatures brought out of a hat. Later, the magician had told him, 'It's just your mind playing tricks on you.' Maybe now his mind was tricking him.

But could the trick be so true, so alive, and around for three weeks, eating meals with you, and coughing that disturbing cough, which jolted Kunaka out of his nightmares every night. So, he continued to go to the bus stop every day, carrying his guitar with him in order to play songs to welcome his son home.

But all things come to an end and all things must converge into some sort of truth. Kunaka, finally believing he was mad and that illusion was truth, was found sitting next to his bedridden youngest son and grandchildren, holding his guitar as if strumming a mournful tune. He was dead.

God's Will

FOR MOST, THE FARMS WERE THE PLACES people went to escape the poverty that had haunted their existence in the town locations and sandy reserves. In fact, some briefly succeeded in their emancipation, pouncing upon the wealth left by white farmers who were fleeing the war vets sent to drive them out. We also went there, to escape the ugly stares and sneers of our neighbours after Cathy had fallen ill, and everyone whispered that she had AIDS. She was only a child. The farm offered us the solace of being unknown among strangers; but despite all our hopes, Cathy died. We buried her on a rainy Saturday morning. The elderly among us said it wasn't a bad omen but rather meant that she had been accepted into heaven.

'Her body is too small for her age,' the doctor said on the day we got her into hospital, fifty-two kilometers away from our farm. Of course, we already knew that, at fifteen she had the body of an eight year old.

'She was born frail,' was all we told him. We dared not tell him anything else about her troubled existence. Such memories had been relegated to the hidden drawer in our family cupboard; now they threatened to resurface and haunt us again.

And when the doctor insisted that we tell him her medical history, every-one looked at me, imploring me to open those drawers that carried our dirty linen. I could not meet their eyes as we stood surrounding the small hospital bed, and my eyes filled with tears.

She must have had been about four months old when she first became ill with severe diarrhoea. We were told that it was because she was teething, feeling foolish when the elderly nurse said, "Who doesn't know that diarrhoea is a normal symptom in teething babies."

43

'Pneumonia followed diarrhoea. The n'anga liked to attend to people right under his verandah in broad daylight. Four streets met right in front of his doorstep. "Good marketing technique," he told us, "And it shows that nothing is wrong with our African medicine."

'Many, like us, went to church, and wouldn't be seen doing things of the dark, but we always visited the herbalist at night so no one would see us. Despite that, at the end of it all, I knew everyone who visited him. Who wouldn't after visiting him for two years for the treatment of illnesses that no one could name? Sometimes we took her to hospital.

'Cathy, however, was determined to live. She outgrew her ailments and started going to school. It was a marvel to see how she played with the other children and made them laugh. But she was smaller than all of them. Her body never caught up with her age.'

But now, when I look back upon it all, I see that doing good is not a choice one can make deliberately, rather we all have an equal dosage of good in us. And the longer one stays on this earth, the more likely we are to exhaust the good we have. It is only in being bad that we have a choice.

'Sometimes Cathy would leave her friends outside and join me. She would pore over my university books tracking the small print with her fingers through squinted eyes: her poor sight was just another consequence of her repeated illness.

'I would chase her out but she would return, push my books aside, and ask me to tell her a story. Sometimes her aunt would help me out; my sister was a fearsome but loving mother to both her two daughters and the frail little girl.'

'Where is her mother?' The doctor asked prompting my rambling disquisition.

We looked at each other then my sister responded, 'She died.'

'Sorry.' The doctor muttered, putting the stethoscope to Cathy's small chest.

'And the father, where is he?'

'He died too.' I replied.

The doctor said nothing more, but we stood there, transfixed, waiting for him to say something: anything. He scribbled something on the patient's card for the young nurse who waited patiently beside him absentmindedly humming a political party jingle.

Then the doctor playfully tickled Cathy, 'How are you?' he asked

She smiled and replied that she was well. The doctor smiled and moved on to the next patient, another frail child who had rarely stopped coughing since we arrived.

I did not return to the farm with everyone else. I kept vigil and in the following days, I watched my niece slowly waste away, while I sat by her bedside, angry that I could not do anything to help her. As if she understood, she would place her hand in mine saying, 'Sekuru, pray for me.' My prayers were silent, and then I would ask her to say the rosary, and she would do so, labouring over each sentence and bead but never leaving anything out.

'What is it, muzukuru?' I would ask whenever the silence had become too great for me to bear.

'It's God's will, Sekuru,' she always replied.

I wondered whether she knew what she meant. But I knew that it was indeed God's will that she be born of sick parents at a time when the plague was still a myth and everyone accused witches of any illness that befell us.

We struggled to fathom what had possessed her at such an early an age that she be always sick. But no exorcism could drive the devil out of her blood, not even when we knew every n'anga and prophet in our location, and city.

Her father died when she was about six years old. We mourned very little of him. He had abandoned her mother soon after the child's birth and gone on to remarry. But his death, and that of his new wife and child, of an illness that we did not recognise, meant nothing in our family or our niece's young life. 'Serves him right,' we said when my sister, Cathy's mother, was out of earshot: 'He thought he could get away with wasting people's daughters.'

But whatever had eaten Cathy's father came to devour her mother exactly four years later and with the same hungry speed. At the hospital, they said it was TB 2, 'curable', but still she died and we buried her in December, exactly two days after her daughter's tenth birthday.

For three days, we mourned for Cathy's mother. 'Would the ground ever tire of eating us up?' Now it was taking away all the young people, leaving orphans and the aged. Who would bury the old people when they died? Who could work to feed the hungry children? The questions were too many for our weak hearts. What consoled us was that at least our sister had left a daughter to remind us of her.

But if she looked anything like her mother all that remained of the likeness were her gleaming, sunken eyes, just like those of our sister just before she died.

I had come to treasure Cathy's short fragile life over the years when we had come so close to losing her. I was afraid that if she were to die, she would take with her part of my soul. Perhaps I wanted her to remain alive more for me than for her.

With this realisation, I started crying. It was Cathy who raised her hand and wiped away the tears on my cheeks.

'What is it, *Sekuru*?' She asked her voice not more than a whisper.

'It's God's will, Cathy.' I replied, unsure of whether I knew what those words meant after all, but she smiled faintly.

The next morning, my family came in from the farm and we all went to the hospital. The nurses told us that Cathy had cried through the night. I went to her bed and found her staring vacantly into space. She did not look at me when I called her name.

We stood around her, not knowing what to do or what to say to each other. We were afraid that we could say the wrong things, as if her life was hanging on our tongues, like the words we lose every time we talk.

'*Sekuru.*'

'Yes, Cathy.' I replied moving closer.

'Why must I die?' She was still looking into space as if already at something that we could not see ourselves.

Everyone looked away. I did not know what to say. But I had to say something. Her aunt left the ward overwhelmed.

'You won't die if you take your pills.' I said taking her hand in mine.

'Won't you just let me go? *Mhama* is calling me to come to her.'

'No. Because we love you.' I gently squeezed the child's arm and she looked at me. 'Now no more nonsense about dying or I will call auntie to beat you up,' I said trying to sound light-hearted, but my words were hollow.

'Are you angry with me, *Sekuru*?'

'Of course, not,' I replied.

Then tell me a story to carry into my dream, she said.

I told her her favourite story. The one about her grandfather's drunken escapades and boxing exploits in the big city of Harare. By the time I'd finished, she was sleeping soundly, her mouth drawn into what could have been a smile. But that afternoon, she again refused to take her medication and we had to send for the priest. She refused to join us in the rosary.

That night I could not sleep, thinking of what she might be undergoing. I tossed and turned saying silent prayers. I felt empty, robbed of all emotion. I thought of the coughing child I'd not seen that morning and realised that my niece was not alone in the struggle against the plague.

I had met many children borne of sick parents, children who were born with the curse of the devil, the plague that was finishing us up. It was in their blood. But their plight had never meant anything to me. Now I wondered how many of them would end up on death's bed, dying slowly, too dazed to understand what was happening to them, begging to die when children their age were beginning to learn what life was all about.

Even as I walked into hospital early that morning, I knew that Cathy had left us, but I did not tell the others. It was at 3 a.m., the elderly nurse told us sympathetically. But I knew she was just doing her duty, and before she turned into the next ward, she would be laughing at how I, a man, stupidly let out a long wail ahead of all the women.

After all, death is God's will, isn't it?

The Third Trek — Resettling

THE DRIVER OF THE POLICE TRUCK WAS impatient with *mhama* who kept insisting we use the beaten down track we'd used when we came in the scotch cart. *Mhama* told him that if we went on a different road then she would not know the way back home. I don't know why she lied, because when we came to the farm, she'd told *baba* that the bigger road was less bumpy. Of course, *baba* told her to shut up because he doesn't take instructions from anyone. I don't know whether he will accept that the farm is no longer ours. I pray that he will because I don't want to go back to there again. There's no school and I have to spend all the days playing with Chido. I no longer want to play with her. She's just a girl. I am now a big boy. Also, the farms have made *mhama* bad, and there is no priest to make her good.

Mhama has changed a lot. She argued with the driver and he ended up taking the rutted track. I thought the police were more fearful than *baba* because they carried their big guns and wore metal hats. *Baba* only carried the gun, which he found in the *murungu's* bedroom, when he went out to hunt wild animals. He always sold the meat but never brought the money home.

The other police officers who sat in the back with us laughed and joked all the way home. I don't know if they were laughing at *mhama* who was sitting with Chido in her lap staring stubbornly at the road behind us or at the driver who kept popping his head out of his window and cursing the bad road. But I know *mhama* has become strong now and no matter how they laugh, they won't hurt her.

In fact, I think *mhama* won. We had a puncture along the way and everyone started cursing *mhama*, but she only smiled and remained in her seat, ignoring the scorching sun. I was helped down to pee and so was Chido; afterwards, she got in the way of the men changing the tyre and they threatened to beat her up. Then she started wailing so loudly that I had to put my hands over my ears.

Chido can be a pain. *Mhama* ignored her even when a policeman shouted, '*Shut her up. Shut that child up, will you?*' I didn't know that policemen can also be bad to children. I thought they only frightened old people who have taken other people's things.

Then, just after we'd set off again, *mhama* ordered the driver to stop so that she could visit the bush. The driver was so infuriated that he threatened to drop us before we got to the house, and he did. I think the policemen sitting with us were hungry because they were no longer talking and laughing but wore sullen faces. But when *mhama* gave Chido and me food, she did not offer any to them. I think this was because they were bad to Chido and kept laughing at *mhama*, like she was Hingiro, the fool.

I once asked *baba* why people always laughed when Hingiro was around and he said it was because he was *sichupeti*. Baba uses a lot of English words – that's what he said the *murungu's* language is called. I never liked the way *baba* said 'sichupeti' even when he scolded *mhama*. I began to hate the policemen for laughing that way at her.

The sun had already set when we arrived and the driver would not take us up to our huts. That time, I think the driver won because for once *mhama* cursed, but the driver said he would not go one inch further. So, the policemen started taking our things out of the truck while *mhama* kept cursing, and yelling at them to take due care. I'd never heard *mhama* curse this much before.

All that is two years ago now. I know that because I can now count, 'one, two, three…' I have been going to school again and the other children sometimes tease me because I am older than them. There are not many children in our village any more. *Mhama* says that they went to the farms with their parents. I wonder if there are any schools where they are.

The headman came to see us the morning after we came home. He told *mhama* that we could no longer stay at our house. He said that he had sold the fields to someone because *baba* had told him that we were not coming back. *Mhama* must have still been angry with the policemen because she only looked at the headman like he was *sichupeti* and told him to leave her alone.

I think the headman is mad. How could he ever listen to what *baba* says? You see, *mhama* still has the plaster cast on her hand and she kept lifting it menacingly and banging it on the armrest of her chair. The headman left quietly. Even now that her hand is healed, he never talks about the fields. I wonder why he told *mhama* that he'd sold the fields because no one ever came to claim them afterwards. I think *mhama* is scary now.

Mhama took a lot of things from the *murungu's* house. So many, we do not even use some of them. She made people repair our old huts and gave them chipped china plates, old clothes and other things she didn't care about. She always made people feel like she was the one losing the most from the deal. Now, our home is better than all the others in the village. I tell the other children about my bed which used to be the *murungu's* child's bed. If they do not believe me, I show them the pictures of the murungu's children playing on it. I still have them.

We have two new cows now. I don't know who brought them. I only came back from school and found the big cabinet, which *mhama* had brought with us, gone and in its place two big cows. I think the person must have found the cattle on the farms because they're bigger than all the other cattle in the village. Now, I sometimes herd cattle with the other boys and *mhama* promised me that we'll have goats very soon. She tells me that I am the man of the house now, and everything will be mine one day.

I am thinking of all these things now because I didn't go to school today. *Mhama* woke me up and I told her that I was not feeling well. In fact, I'm not. I'm angry. You see I might no longer be the man here any more. *Baba* came back last night. He stank of beer and could hardly stand. I don't even know who told him that we were back home.

He just stumbled in, and for some time we all sat there, not moving. The light was dim; the paraffin lamp *mhama* brought with her has not been re-filled. *Mhama* says that the whole country has no paraffin. I don't believe her. I don't know how big a country is, but our village and the farm are all big. How can she say that something bigger than all the villages and farms has no paraffin? I think she just doesn't have anything more to exchange for the fuel.

And then *baba* asked us if we had not seen him. He was wriggling like a drunk man. I just continued munching my roasted maize-cob. I wasn't impressed. Chido must not have known who he was because she just walked

50

over to him and peered into his face, then she pulled a face and stepped backwards. She was just in time because *baba* had stretched out his dirty hands to embrace her. That was when everything went bad. Chido does not like strangers and she started wailing. You see, she hasn't outgrown crying and *mhama*, who doesn't care much any more, tells her that she can weep as much as she likes. *Baba* was infuriated. But it was *sichupeti!* How could he expect Chido to remember him. And even if she did, his breath was smelling very bad.

Then *baba* slapped Chido on the cheek and *mhama*, who had been watching him, suddenly stood up and placed herself between *baba* and Chido. She has never stood up to him before, but that was because she used to go to church. Since we came home, *mhama* has never visited the old priest. In fact, she sent word that she would have nothing to do with him or the church any more, and someone must have told him to take her word for it.

Despite his anger, *baba* looked frail. He wobbled as he stood and then he pushed *mhama* but she did not move a centimetre. He got angrier, Chido wailed some more, and I munched on my maize cob praying that *mhama* would pummel *baba* to death. I didn't want him around us any longer.

Then *mhama* pushed *baba* and he fell back onto the bench that runs across half the kitchen hut. I dropped the cob, ready to cheer like we did when the bulls fought in the pastures. But *mhama* only hit *baba* once with her hand and then he feigned sleep. I could not believe it. *Baba* is clever: he started snoring even as *mhama* was about to pound him again.

I was angry at *mhama*. Chido kept wailing and I wanted to beat her up. I think I now hate everyone, specially grown-ups. Why did *mhama* just stop there, her hand in mid-air; she could have hit *baba* again. Instead, she started weeping. I don't know why. She then turned to Chido and threatened to beat her up if she didn't shut up.

Baba continued snoring. He was drunk but still *mhama* took him in her arms and carried him to their sleeping hut. She is stronger than he is. I don't even know what they were still doing there until late into the morning. But *mhama* was happy when they woke up, and *baba* was sober.

Now I am here alone and angry. They have all gone to the fields to inspect the maize crop. *Mhama* must have brought some clothes for *baba* from the farm because he has changed into clean trousers and is wearing new boots. *Baba* and *mhama* carried their big hoes on their shoulders and Chido held *baba's* hand. He must not be strong enough to carry her yet. But I don't want to shake his hand.

I no longer know what to expect. Before they left for the fields, *mhama* killed the cock that she told me last week was mine. I refused to eat it. And then she went to the kraals, showing *baba* the same cattle that she had told me were mine, all the time saying, 'I got these for you'. And *baba* was grinning and nodding and saying, 'You were wise to take all those things from the farm.'

I want to laugh because I think *mhama* is *sichupeti* but only tears flow from my eyes. Now it seems that neither *baba* or *mhama* even care to look at me. I wish I was back at the farm and I would have run away to *sekuru*. I don't care about anything any more and I know what I will do while they are away. I will burn the *murungu's* children's pictures because they will remind me of the bed, when *mhama* decides that she wants to exchange it for some more cattle or bricks to build a house like the *murungu's*. She carried many zinc roofing sheets when we came in the police truck. In fact, their house looked like it had been picked by white ants.